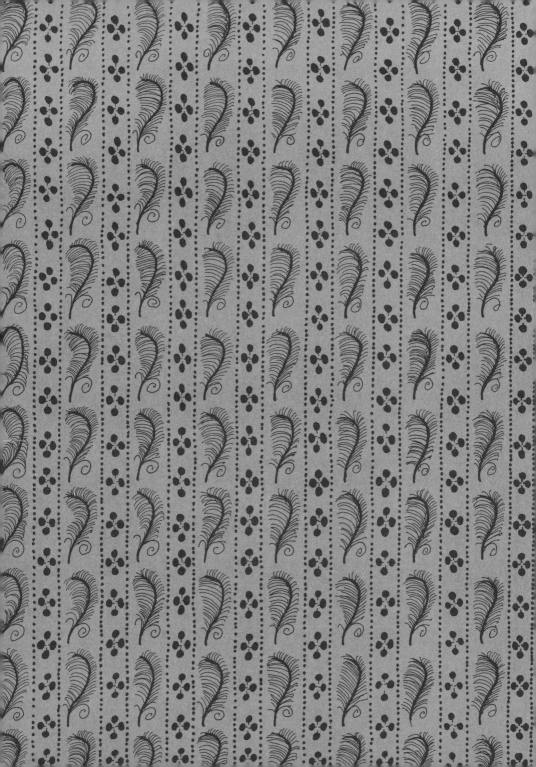

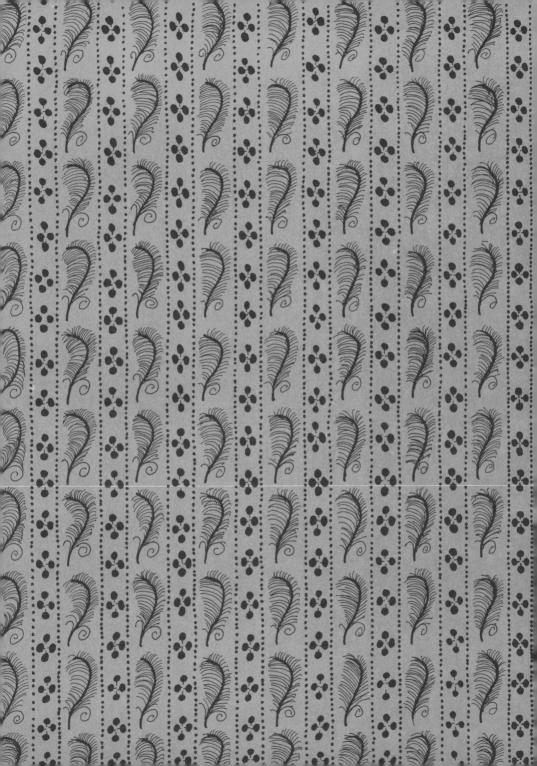

THERE GOES FEATHERTOP!

A changeling version of
Nathaniel Hawthorne's "Feathertop"

THERE GOES FEATHERTOP!

by Norma Farber

illustrated by Marc Brown

A Unicorn Book   E. P. Dutton   New York

Library of Congress Cataloging in Publication Data

Farber, Norma.   There goes feathertop!
(A Unicorn book)

SUMMARY: When the witch's scarecrow comes to
life, Miss Polly Gookin takes a shine to him.
[1. Scarecrows—Fiction.   2. Stories in rhyme]
I. Brown, Marc Tolon.   II. Title.
PZ8.3.F224Tg   [E]   78-12096   ISBN: 0-525-29667-0

Published in the United States by E. P. Dutton, a Division
of Sequoia-Elsevier Publishing Company, Inc., New York

Published simultaneously in Canada by Clarke,
Irwin & Company Limited, Toronto and Vancouver

Editor: Emilie McLeod   Designer: Riki Levinson

Printed in the U.S.A.   First Edition
10 9 8 7 6 5 4 3 2 1

For Hiram and Ethelyne—
exactly as they are

THERE GOES FEATHERTOP,
lifelike as can be!
Mother Rigby made him
for all the world to see.

She started with a broomstick,
a handle and a rung
to which was tied a ruler,
near which a rod was hung.

So now he has a backbone,
two legs and both his arms.
Mother Rigby adds a bag
of straw and witch's charms.

Crown him with a pumpkin!
How fine the fellow grows:
holes for eyes, slit for mouth,
bluish knob for nose.

"I've seen on human shoulders
some faces worse," she said.
"And many a proper gentleman
holds up a pumpkin head.

"Don't you cry, my muffin.
You'll like my cunning plan.
If rubbish makes a scarecrow,
then clothes will make the man!"

The coat: plum-colored satin,
once costly, sleek and rare;
but ancient now, in tatters,
and patched beyond repair.

Its breast once bore a medal.
A hole is all that shows:
an empty star whose owner
has vanished. Where? Who knows?

The waistcoat: faded velvet,
a triumph in its day,
embroidered once with golden threads
that now are musty gray.

The breeches: dimmest scarlet,
gaping at every seam.
Stockings: the like of cobwebs,
substantial as a dream.

"And now a wig for fashion:
my dear dead husband's own.
A tricorn, topped with feather.
How elegant you've grown!

"Here's my pipe; start puffing.
The stem's a perfect fit.
More smoke! More smoke! Keep puffing!
Your life depends on it!

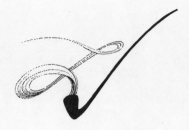

"Well puffed, my lad! Another!
For that's my magic art.
A good strong whiff, a mouthful
inhaled with all your heart!

"You see? You feel more lively,
the deeper down you puff!
Let smoke bewitch you into life
by blowing rings enough!

"You see? My pipelet demons
dance round and round the bowl!
All you need is deepdrawn breath
and freshly lighted coal!

"Ha! ha! my roguish fellow!
Ready to step outdoors?
I've made you nearly human.
Go forth! The world is yours!

"Go forth, I say, you patchwork,
you clump of rags and sticks;
you pumpkin-head, keep puffing,
you bag of witch's tricks!"

THERE GOES FEATHERTOP!
A fine effect he makes.
His figure looks more dazzling
with every breath he takes.

The people crowd around him.
They bow and call him Sir—
except one squalling little child
and one mean skulking cur.

He visits Justice Gookin,
by whom he's well received.
The radiance of his person,
once seen, must be believed.

He meets Miss Polly Gookin,
dear prize of heart's desire.
The glowing pumpkin's glowing pipe
has set her heart afire.

She's thrilled to meet the stranger.
Her fanciest gown she wears,
her laciest cap, her jewels,
her fan, her prettiest airs.

With dainty grace she takes his arm.
They stroll, now to, now fro.
The imps careen around his pipe.
His star, his buckles glow.

Pumpkin and Poll, they promenade.
She finds him noble, pure,
a thoroughgoing gentleman.
Her father's not so sure.

A splendid match they seem to make.
A perfect pair they are:
she with her simple comeliness,
he with his fiery star.

She tosses at the looking-glass
a glance as they go by.
She shrieks and sinks upon the floor.
The mirror does not lie.

He halts, he searches in the glass.
Pumpkin, and sticks, and string—
he sees himself for what he is:
a wretched, ragged thing.

A wretched, ragged, ruined thing;
a sham, and nothing more.
He pulls the pipe from pumpkin-slit,
dashes it to the floor.

THERE GOES FEATHERTOP—
back to the witch's door.
"Make me a scarecrow, Mother Rigby,
such as I was before!

"Set me at peace upon a field
    where corn abundant grows,
    where I may make the children laugh,
    and hardly scare the crows."

NORMA FARBER took a Hawthorne tale, her special talent for rhyme and rhythm, and like Mother Rigby came up with her own creation. This imaginative verse-story about a scarecrow is a product of her New England background, her sense of drama, and her skill and experience as a poet and translator.

MARC BROWN made his first playmates out of broomsticks and newspaper and went on to furnish his parents' living room with paper people. He lives in a nineteenth-century house in Hingham, Massachusetts, and collects the antique baskets, clocks, and candlesticks which provide background for this nineteenth-century tale. His pen and ink drawings are in the style of schoolbook etchings and the silhouettes fashionable in that period.

The title is set in Gallia; other display type is Palatino foundry. The text is set in Garamond Alphatype. The book was printed by offset at Rae Publishing Company.

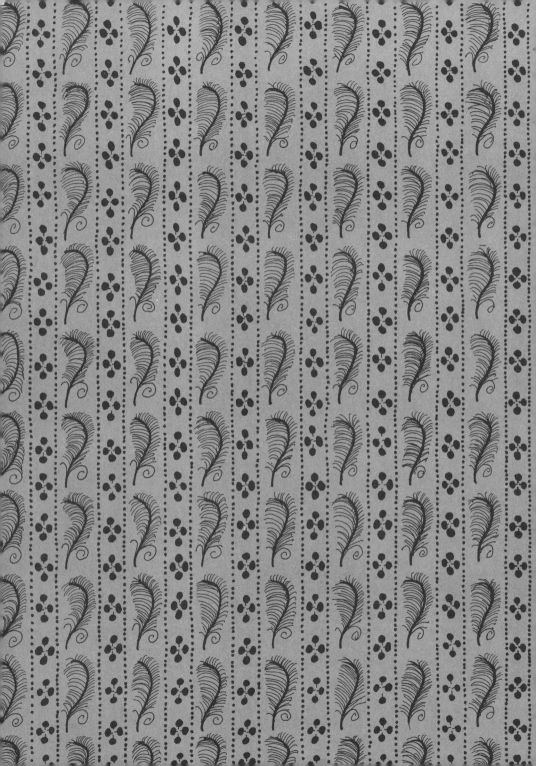

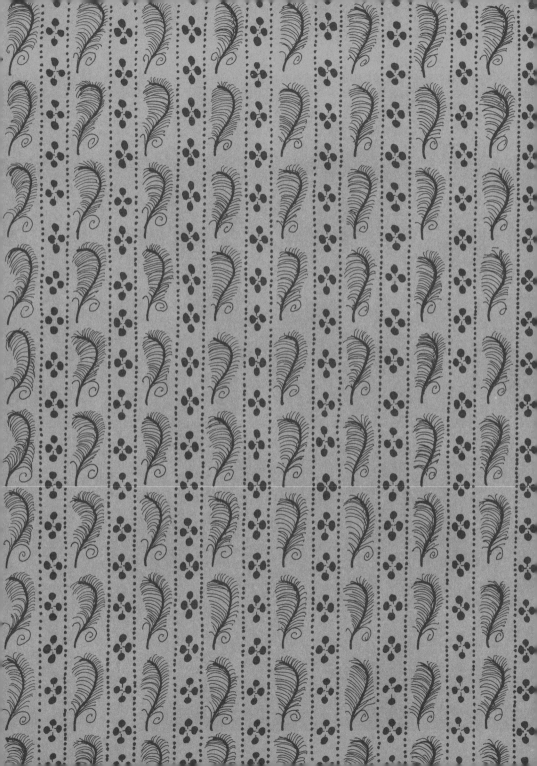